For permission requests, email to the publisher

mmandiDESIGNS
www.immandidesigns @ gmail.com

Printed in the United States of America

STAINED GLASS WINDOWS

Genesis 2: 2-3

"And on the seventh day God finished his work that he had done, and he rested on the seventh day from all his work that he had done. So God blessed the seventh day and made it holy, because on it God rested from all his work that he had done in creation."

A Ω

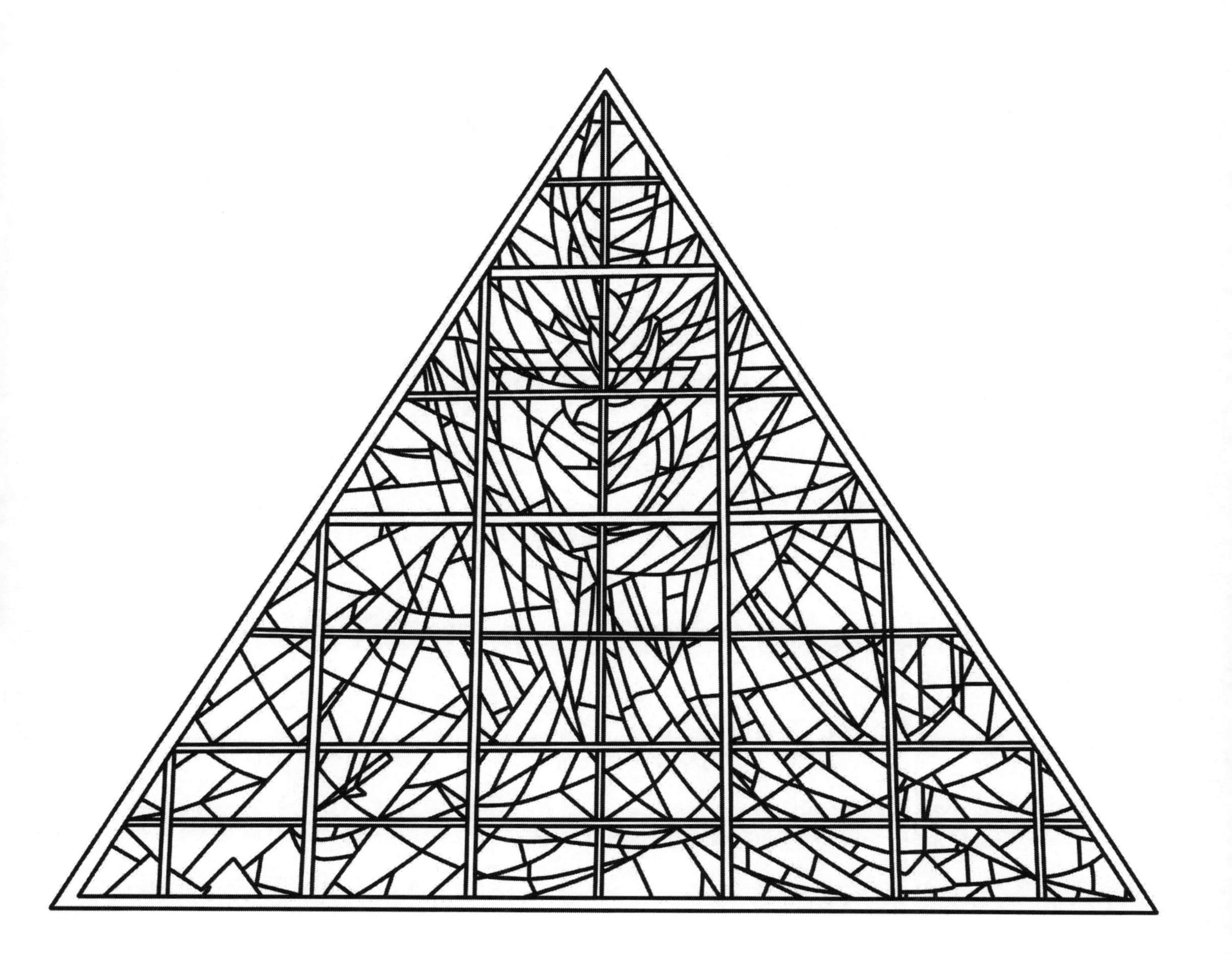

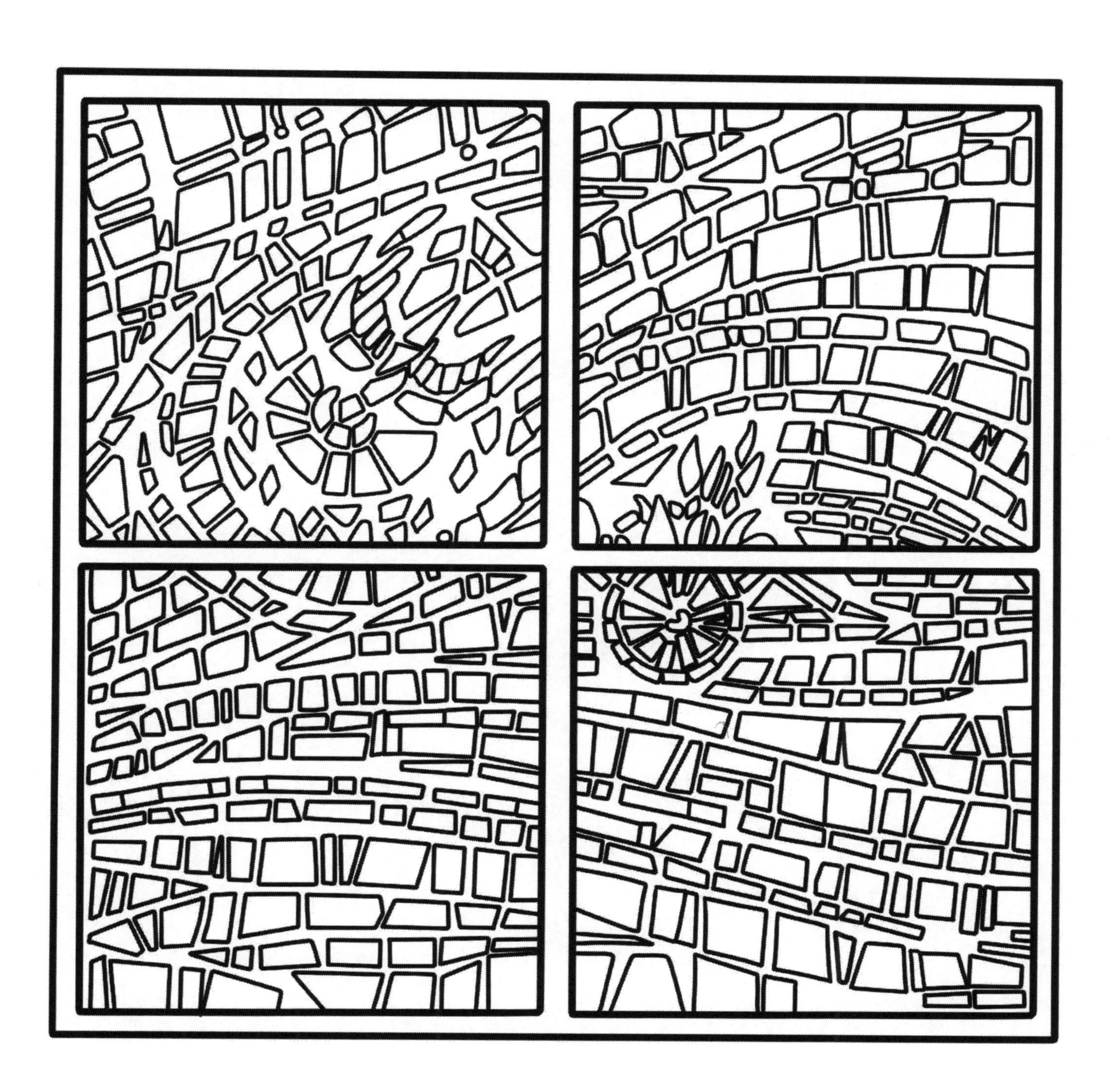

S • JOANNES

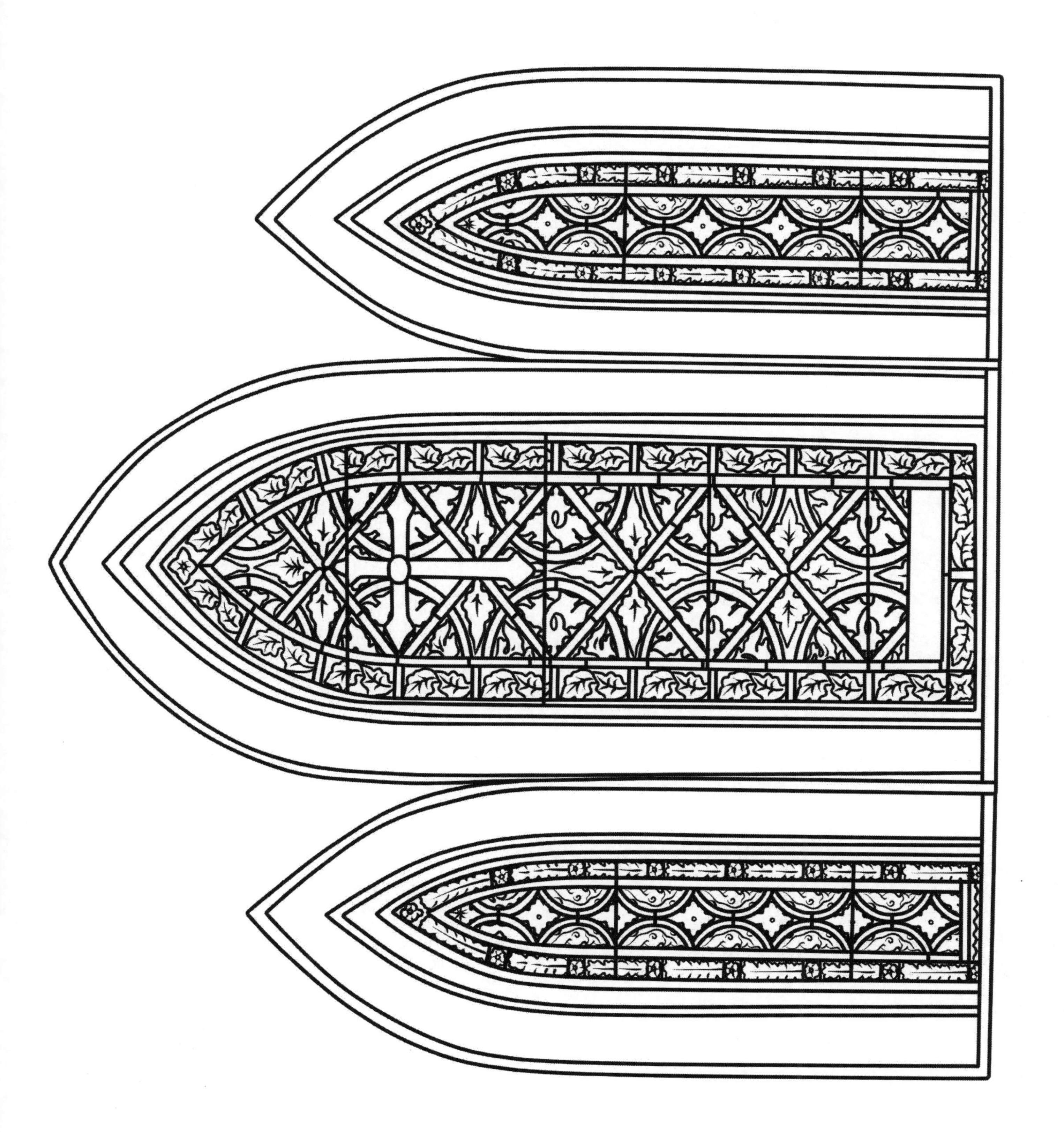

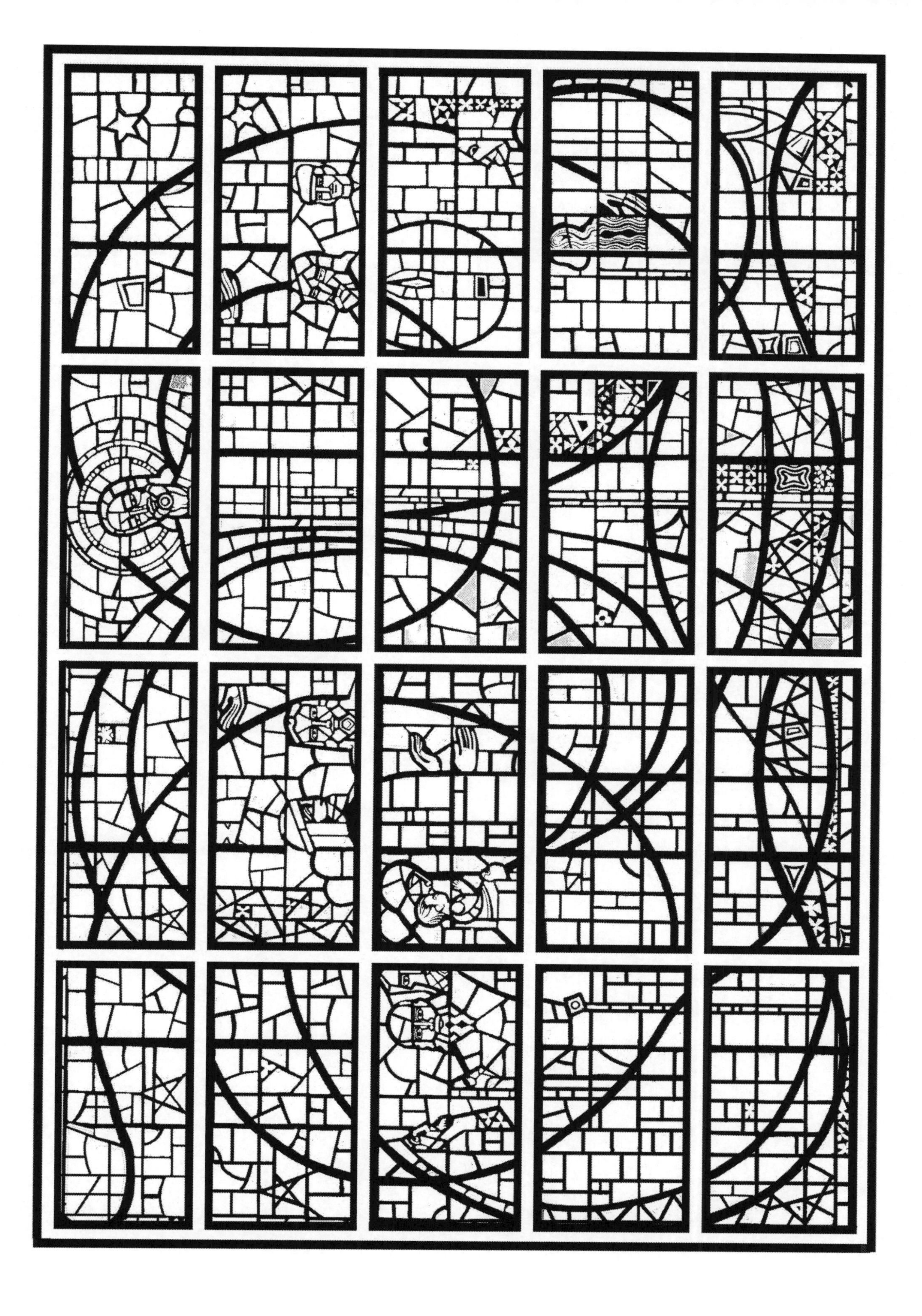

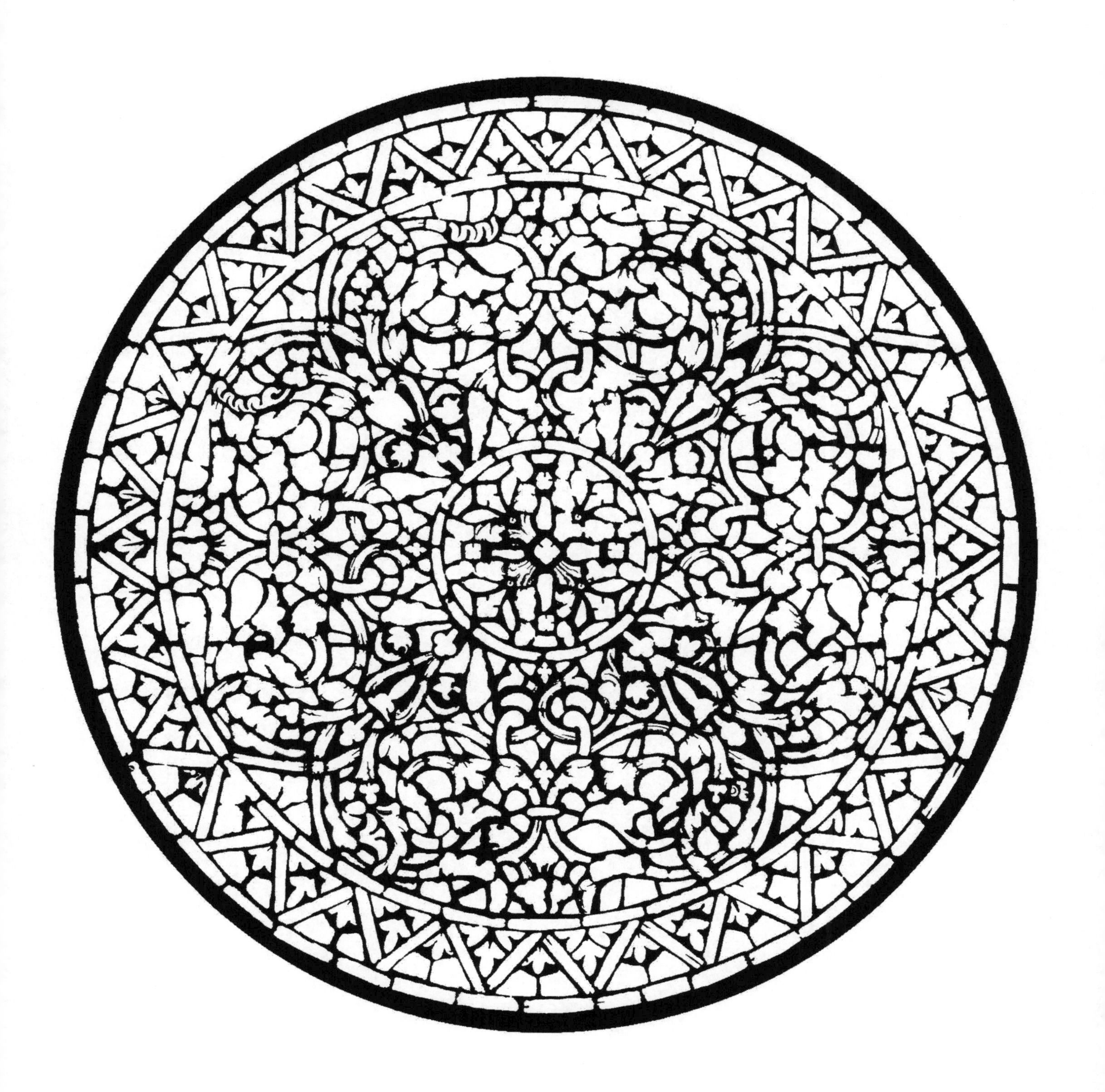

The Stations of the Cross

A 14-step Catholic devotion that commemorates Jesus Christ's last day on Earth as a man. The 14 devotions, or stations, focus on specific events of His last day, beginning with His condemnation. The stations are commonly used as a mini pilgrimage as the individual moves from station to station. At each station, the individual recalls and meditates on a specific event from Christ's last day. Specific prayers are recited, then the individual moves to the next station until all 14 are complete.

The Stations of the Cross are commonly found in churches as a series of 14 small icons or images. They can also appear in church yards arranged along paths. The stations are most commonly prayed during Lent on Wednesdays and Fridays, and especially on Good Friday, the day of the year upon which the events actually occurred.

1st Station: *Jesus is condemned to death*

2nd Station: Jesus carries His cross

Jesus falls the first time

4th Station: Jesus meets his mother

5th Station: Simon of Cyrene helps Jesus to carry his cross

Veronica wipes the face of Jesus

7th Station: Jesus falls the second time

8th Station: Jesus meets the women of Jerusalem

9th Station: Jesus falls a third time

10th Station: Jesus clothes are taken away

11th Station: Jesus is nailed to the cross

12th Station: Jesus dies on the cross

13th Station: The body of Jesus is taken down from the cross

14th Station: Jesus is laid in the tomb

Made in the USA
Middletown, DE
11 July 2019